RETURN
TO THE
GLASS MENAGERIE

Circa 1877. Depicted as 'The Big White House On A Hill' in The Glass Menagerie.

A Tribute to Tennessee Williams.

CONTENTS

Foreword

A Tribute to Tennessee Williams

In a big white house on a hill in Blue Mountain, Mississippi, sits the fictional residence of Tennessee Williams's famed delusional southern belle, Amanda Wingfield. I discovered his characters from the play, *The Glass Menagerie*, continuing their lives long after the world-renowned playwright's demise.

My 1877 historic Greek Revival big white house, the role model for Amanda's home, sits grandly on Hutchins Hill in Blue Mountain, Mississippi, population 920. The home remains prominently in the town of Blue Mountain immortalized by the famous playwright, Tennessee Williams, a native Mississippian, in his first play, *The Glass Menagerie*, premiering in 1944. It is still performed around the world as one of the most significant plays in the American Theater cannon to gain commercial and artistic success.

I fell truly, madly, deeply in love-at-first-sight with the imposing historic big white house on a hill in August 2016, signing a contract to call it home.

I was the first non-family member to reside at 'Hutchins House' since 1887. It was to be a long dusty road reviving this faded architectural beauty in Mississippi's crown on a budget. The home was built in 1877. The renovation was due to interior and exterior restoration beyond its remaining breath-taking facade.

After residing at Hutchins House for two years, it dawned on me this is the only big white house on a hill in Blue Mountain–exactly the spot Tennessee Williams chose for his famous southern belle, Amanda Wingfield. I started yearning to revive the celebrated characters in the award-winning play–bringing them home again to give them another chance to recover their losses.

Williams great "memory play" references the big white house on a hill in Blue Mountain, Mississippi, where Amanda Wingfield entertained "over seventeen gentleman callers every Sunday afternoon." The huge cadre of gentleman callers called regularly hoping to woo her—to win her fickle heart—to claim the most sought-after belle in the big white house on a hill.

The world-famous Morgan Library & Museum in Manhattan showcased Blue Mountain,

Mississippi, during their "No Refuge but Writing' tribute to Tennessee Williams in 2018. Dozens of references were displayed of Amanda Wingfield's days growing up in Blue Mountain. Actress Laurette Taylor's renowned line from the original Broadway play (1944) was "When I was a girl in Blue Mountain I led the cotillion, I won the cake walk prize, and wore this dress to the Governor's Ball, when I was a girl in Blue Mountain." Mississippi Heights Academy was founded for boys in Blue Mountain in 1904. Many of her Delta-born "gentleman callers" came from the school.

May you enjoy the continuation of the fictional fate of Amanda, Tom, and Laura Wingfield's return to Mississippi from the St. Louis tenement where they were abandoned as much as I delighted in bringing all of them back "home" to Blue Mountain, Mississippi.

With love, appreciation, and deep admiration for my fellow Mississippian, Thomas Lanier Williams, renowned as, *Tennessee Williams.*

Prologue

AMANDA WINGFIELD'S floral dress with its "fit and flare" skirt billowed in the early Spring breeze as she sat in an old wooden porch swing impatiently awaiting the first of her huge cadre of gentleman callers, anxious to woo her – win her fickle heart–to claim the most sought after southern belle who lived in the big white house on a hill in Blue Mountain, Mississippi.

Suddenly, she shouted, "Mama, I'm going to pick some more daffodils for the parlor!" "A few more?" her incredulous Mama called back, realizing dozens of bouquets were already in place.

The flowers are also known as narcissus, meaning a person with a great admiration for themselves. Amanda's youthful vanity rivaled Narcissus, the Greek god who fell in love with his reflection in a lake.

Some suitors came via horse and buggy from the areas surrounding Blue Mountain: Cotton Plant, Ripley, Walnut, Falkner, and Tiplersvile; other young men hailed from the Mississippi Delta: Yazoo City, Natchez, Clarksdale, and Greenwood. The young Delta hopefuls were close by attending Mississippi Heights Academy in Blue Mountain, a strict boys' school within walking distance to Amanda's grand hillside home.

Amanda's coquettish charm was legendary; her good looks and mannerisms were inherited from her maternal grandmother, Maxine 'Max' Lafayette Hutchins, a legend in her day.

Amanda's closest childhood friend and suitor, Waymon Cother, known for his ardor and devotion to Amanda, was considered a favorite for her hand in marriage. He confided to his sister, Sarah Emma, a fine pianist, "Sarah Emma, Amanda is the only girl in the world for me." Sarah Emma silently despaired, hoping her only brother wouldn't be disappointed by this immature butterfly-of-a-girl he adored.

After a busy Sunday afternoon with more than a dozen gentleman callers arriving to charm Amanda, she went to bed early looking forward to a trip to downtown Blue Mountain for a visit to the mercantile and general store where her family kept an open bill for charges to be paid monthly. Her special stop was to purchase more ribbons for her hair and hats plus, a fried pie known in the South as "crab lanterns" due to a filling of crab apples wrapped in fried dough with slits resembling a lantern. She loved all the attention from merchants and friends as she slowly meandered downtown.

Even though threats of an impending World War II were spoken, Spring was in the air with sunshine lighting her path down the busy sidewalk. As she exited the mercantile store suddenly, a voice from afar shouted, "Wait, miss! I hope to introduce myself to you!" Turning quickly, she spotted a tall man in a nice three-piece suit trying to get her attention. He was standing next to a shiny new Buick Super automobile never seen in Blue Mountain.

Amanda turned slowly smiling at the stranger while walking toward him.

The shoe salesman from St. Louis captivated Amanda.

"I am Mr. Wingfield, head salesman for a shoe company in St. Louis," he proudly shared.

Amanda was thrilled by the attention from such an exotic person at a chance meeting in her hometown.

Mr. Wingfield immediately planned a secret meeting with Amanda at dusk in the park below her nearby home. "See you later, Mr. Wingfield," Amanda said- as she started uphill to her lovely white house. "I will be waiting," Mr. Wingfield enthused.

As twilight arrived, Amanda told her mother, "Mama, I am going for a quick walk in the park."

She raced downhill toward the picturesque setting to find Mr. Wingfield leaning against the shiny new Buick. He wasted no time gathering her in his arms to kiss her. Amanda was surprised and intrigued. Fifteen minutes later, Mr. Wingfield talked the innocent southern belle into taking a ride with him to St. Louis.

She ran uphill to leave a no te for her family in the quiet entry hall: "I have decided to willingly go to St. Louis with a gentleman for a visit. His name is Mr. Wingfield. He is so mannerly and wants to be friends." Amanda was *en route* downhill and into the new Buick Super within minutes.

Always a dreamy dreamer, she had no time to retract her ill-fated reckless decision. She was ill-prepared for arriving at a tenement in a lower-class area of St. Louis near a shoe factory with a fire escape entrance.

Wingfield smoothly placated Amanda, "Honey, this is a temporary place due to my busy travel schedule."

Despair and impoverishment knocked on the shabby apartment door daily, bringing no pleasure to the young woman. Mr. Wingfield, the traveling salesman, was on the road again in one week after he forced her to marry him forever by saying her family in Blue Mountain would never welcome her home again. Much to her horror, she found herself pregnant and alone. Her constant mantra to the errant husband was, "Please don't leave me here alone."

A healthy baby boy, Tom Wingfield, arrived and was two months old before he met his traveling father. Tom was a handful for Amanda, who grew up with servants taking care of her in Blue Mountain. She tried to love Tom even though she was barely eighteen years old with no experience. Every day she tried to think of ways and means to return to Blue Mountain.

During a short trip back to the tenement, Mr. Wingfield impregnated Amanda again. Wingfield repeatedly told Amanda, "I'll be back home in a few days!" Her son, Tom, was a toddler, and a daughter, Laura soon arrived. As years flew by, Tom became a worker at the shoe factory nearby while Amanda tried in vain to train Laura to be a southern belle.

Laura suffered a childhood illness that left her with a slight limp. She imagined the limp to be far worse than it was.

Amanda's constant criticisms kept Tom running out of sight *via* the fire escape and Laura concentrating on her tiny glass menagerie figurines to pass the time. His mother infuriated him when she had tantrums resulting in tearing his small book collection to pieces, "Mother, please do not destroy, *Lady Chatterley's Lover*, by Mr. D. H. Lawrence–it's almost impossible to find a copy." Amanda roared, "You are not going to read this trash in our home." At the time, Lawrence's book was banned in America.

Laura's unicorn was her favorite creature in her glass menagerie because it was "different," like her. Hours flew by as she entertained herself with the delicate glass creatures. She begged, "Mama, please stop interrupting me! I already know how to be a southern belle like you." The small impoverished household was in a constant state of flux.

Tom secretly made up his troubled mind to run away from St. Louis with a special friend who offered him transportation and lodging in New Orleans. He exited *via* the fire escape never saying goodbye. Tom had become troubled by his coworkers in the shoe factory who depressed him with their constant teasing about his southern belle Mother.

Amanda was left alone, impoverished, and hopeless with Laura.

Chapter 1

DESPAIR and impoverishment continued to knock on the door of the shabby apartment bringing no pleasures for the abandoned Amanda and Laura. She was at her wit's end when early one morning in April after a bad cold snap, the postman delivered a letter from Blue Mountain, Mississippi, to the threadbare dwelling. The letter was impressively written on fine linen stationery with a stylized penmanship similar to Amanda's father's Spenserian method. Amanda finally recognized it was from the bank owned by her devoted gentleman caller from yesteryear, Waymon Cother, a lifelong bachelor from Ripley, Mississippi, minutes away from Blue Mountain.

Amanda was shaking with excitement while opening the ecru-hued letter with an embossed Cother Bank logo, address, and telephone number. She quickly called out to her daughter Laura, "Laura, come here right this minute! Our prayers have been answered. We are going home to our big white house on a hill in Blue Mountain, Mississippi. Laura, startled and crying over her mother's unexpected mood swing was surprised over the turn of events saying, "Oh, Mama, will I see your old friends and our family?"

Amanda carefully opened the letter:

Dearest Amanda,

I recently learned of your son, Tom's unexpected departure from St. Louis to New Orleans.

Your grandmother, Maxine Lafayette, unexpectedly passed away during an influenza epidemic two weeks ago. According to her last will and testament, you are her sole heir. The big white house on the hill, its contents, and a sum of cash and bonds are now to be held in your name.

All your friends and relatives are hoping and praying you will be open to returning to Blue Mountain with your daughter, Laura, to reside among people who still love and miss you.

Please let me know via a collect telephone call to my office as soon as possible. My sister, Sarah Emma, and I are standing by to come to St. Louis in our comfortable Woodie station wagon to bring you and Laura home.

In Friendship Forever,

Waymon

Suddenly, with a whoop of joy, Amanda embraced Laura for the first time since Tom's departure.

"Laura, start packing your glass menagerie, my sweet girl, we are going home." Laura's constant fears evaporated, "Mama, this is an answer to our prayers."

The Cothers, along with a certain group of Mississippians loved to resurrect the past: Who's Who; Who's Kin; Religious Affiliations, etc., all deftly woven with expert story-telling. The return of Amanda Wingfield would be the hottest topic in the county.

The Cothers were five hours away from St. Louis within a day after hearing from Amanda. They loaded her few possessions as Amanda and Laura took turns crying with joy immediately departing for Blue Mountain. Lively reminiscences with laughter and tears ensuing continued as the happy passengers traveled south toward home. "Amanda, do you remember always wanting to spend the night at our home in Ripley? You loved it when Sarah Emma read, "The Swish of the Curtain" as a bedtime story while you consumed many homemade cookies with milk."

Sarah Emma said, "I have the book in our library to give to Laura for her children." It was kind even though none of them anticipated Laura being sought after by gentlemen callers. They scheduled a rest stop before heading into Memphis to dine at Anderton's Restaurant, popular since opening in 1913.

Amanda did not want the Cothers' to know how hungry she and Laura were as the miles passed.

After the long drive, the station wagon finally delivered Amanda and Laura to Amanda's 1877 Greek Revival big white house on a hill in Blue Mountain, Mississippi. Amanda quietly thought of her glory days there as the town's darling. The mother and daughter laughed and cried tears of joy when they saw the home untouched by time.

The Cothers' finally departed for their Ripley home about six miles away saying, "We will return in the morning. Plenty of food is in the outside dining room and the pantry." Sarah Emma will bring our housekeeper, Moe, and her favorite grandson, Henry, to help with anything you need.

The Mother and daughter stood in the long drive waving and crying happy tears until the Woodie station wagon was rolling down the hill. While the exterior of the beautiful home was untouched; the interior was begging for refurbishing. "My, my, Laura, we'll have to roll up our sleeves to get our home straight and spotlessly clean. You cannot have gentleman callers until the parlor is spruced up." Laura sighed, resigned to her Mama's delusions. "Yes, Mama, we will start tomorrow."

Chapter 2.

A downstairs pocket-sized bedroom with an 1870 American Renaissance walnut bed was where Laura chose to sleep and dream of a chance for a new life right across the street from Blue Mountain College, *circa* 1873.

"This is the prettiest bed I have ever seen, Mama!" Amanda smiled not choosing to tell her that was where her dearest grandmother chose to sleep for decades. "So many children were born in this historic bed. Goodnight, Laura, I really do love you," Amanda whispered.

Amanda chose to sleep nearby in a dusty gilded French daybed often used for naps. Before drifting off to sleep, she smiled as she spotted her grandfather's English partners desk across the illuminated room. Waymon must have lit the gas heaters on the lower floor earlier.

Down the back porch was an outside kitchen with its big original dinner bell to summon everyone at meal times. The only other outside dining room still in use is in historic Natchez, Mississippi.

Both dwellings have a summer canning room behind the dining room and cooking area.

A watershed of remembrances of times past kept Amanda awake. Slipping out of bed early the next morning to make breakfast, Amanda whispered, "It feels so good to be safely home and no longer hungry or afraid."

As she entered the outdoor kitchen at the end of the lower porch gallery, she was delighted to see the refrigerator and cupboards filled with southern-style staples: Luzianne New Orleans Chicory coffee and tea; real cream; White Lily Self-Rising flour and cornmeal; an assortment of homemade jellies and jams-including, muscadine, Mayhew, and rhubarb; grits for long-cooking; sweet butter; fresh large brown eggs; Smithfield country ham and many more delicacies dear to Amanda's palate and heart. Copper and cast-iron skillets and pans were hanging in the same places as in Amanda's childhood.

A wicker tray used in the old days to bring Amanda breakfast in bed came into sight. She beamed as she started to prepare a feast for Laura to be delivered on the tray with lovely linens and her grandmother's French Renaissance sterling silver. Amanda murmured, "Home at last ... as she readied creamy buttered grits with a catspaw biscuit filled with thinly sliced country ham with red-eye gravy for Laura.

A delicate double-handled Dresden cup was filled with coffee, cream, and a dollop of honey from Clay Hill Plantation. The honey was precious because the bees are taken to an almond crop in California every summer.

Amanda delivered the repast with a smile and sweet, "Good Morning, Laura, this is the same tray my Mama used to bring my breakfast years ago. Enjoy everything and meet me in the outdoor kitchen after you dress." Amanda's usually unpredictable behavior vanished after being home one night. "Please, Lord, let this last," Laura whispered.

Amanda Wingfield still fit into her large wardrobe left behind before she hastily left Blue Mountain with the brutish Mr. Wingfield. Many frocks would become Laura with a bit of alteration.

Days flew by without incident as old family friends and relatives called to welcome them home.

They were working diligently to make the parlor a receiving area for the continuing flow of cousins, friends, and genteel folks who remained a part of Tippah County, Mississippi, society.

The aging Robert McRaven and his lovely wife, Tranquila, came from her historic 1820-1821 family home, "Summertrees" close by in Red Banks, Mississippi. They brought a basket containing jars of homemade icicle pickles; muscadine jelly and whole pickled okra in brine. Freshly baked tea cakes rested in a linen towel on the side of the basket. Tranquila was close to tears tightly embracing Amanda whispering, "Thank God, you are home, darling friend."

A young man Laura's age, Andrew 'Drew' Crawford, stopped by with a calling card and a small gift that turned out to be identical to the lost broken favorite glass menagerie unicorn Laura had broken in an unfortunate dance with one of Tom's friends in St. Louis. After she shrilled in delight seeing the unicorn, she said, "Oh, Mama, how on earth did he know what I missed most of all?" Amanda shrugged not revealing Waymon Cother told the young gent about the unfortunate dance with her very first gentleman caller, Jim O'Connor. Laura identified with the unicorn she called "a different horse."

"Please come again soon, Drew. Perhaps, we can dance around my glass menagerie." He whispered, "Yes, Laura, I will be back soon," and quietly took his leave. Laura did not have to wait too long for the reappearance of Andrew 'Drew' Crawford, a most eligible interested gentleman caller. He returned within days with another tissue-wrapped gift. Laura gasped as she opened it to see a music box that played Stephen Foster's "Beautiful Dreamer." Drew proffered his hand, –

"May I have this dance, Laura?" Suddenly, Laura lost her look of shyness replacing it with a radiant smile saying, "I would love to be your partner."

Amanda Wingfield strongly but, subtly approved of Drew Warford, Laura's first true gentleman caller interested in this fragile 'girl'. The Crawford family from Ashland had banking interests across Tippah County.

Before Drew departed, he extended an invitation to Amanda asking them to join his family for church and lunch the following Sunday.

Amanda told Laura, "Drew was a perfect gentleman caller. You were most charming, too."

After Drew departed, the McRavens arrived for another visit bringing along Robert Leslie, a witty, mannerly gentleman from Ripley they had known for decades. Robert brought Amanda a 'welcome home' gift, a pair of French porcelain candlesticks featuring hand-painted parrots in vivid colors quipping, "Here's a pair of birds you won't have to feed, Amanda." Drew

Crawford suddenly appeared after the other guests. All Tippah County, Mississippi, natives were bursting with curiosity about Amanda's secretive unexpected return.

Still, no word arrived from Tom dashing their hopes of him joining them in Blue Mountain. Amanda and Laura were hoping their dear friend, Waymon Cother, could find Tom to join them in newly found love and plentitude.

Chapter 3

THE anticipated time arrived for Drew Crawford to call for Amanda and Laura for church and Sunday arrived. It was an encouraging sermon followed by social success at lunch. The Crawfords and Wingfields shared ideal camaraderie.

Lunch served on the family Bernardaud china with their monogram and antique Tiffany Chrysanthemum silver pieces was strictly Southern fare: Fried Chicken; Sweet Potato Casserole; Green Beans Viniagrette; along with Chess Pie was delectable.

As Laura and Amanda departed, they chorused, "What a happy occasion! Please join us soon."

"Soon" turned out to be the following Sunday. The Crawford family arrived on time to be served another delicious lunch of braised bourbon pot roast with baby carrots, parsnips, and tiny new red potatoes in *beurre blanc*. A homemade pecan pie with coffee or tea rounded out a fine meal.

After lunch, Drew suddenly asked for everyone's attention. He withdrew briefly returning with six Baccarat champagne flutes and a chilled bottle of vintage Pol Roger champagne.

"May I propose a special toast to our families uniting? It is sudden and sincere. I have spoken privately to Mrs. Wingfield asking permission to wed my forever love, Laura."

A blue velvet Tiffany's box appeared from his pocket; down on one knee, Drew placed a fiery blue sapphire with diamond baguettes on

Laura's tiny hand as tears streamed down her cheeks. "Yes, Drew. Oh, yes, I will become your wife."

Mrs. Crawford (Lillian) and Amanda, leading a thrilled Laura, retired to the parlor to discuss wedding plans while the gentlemen went to the back lower gallery for Cuban cigars.

Lillian Crawford was a delicate dainty lady with Laura's diminutive frame. "Would you like to see my wedding gown created by renowned designer, Ann Lowe?" she asked. Ann Lowe would later in life make history by creating Jacqueline Bouvier Kennedy's wedding gown. Lillian's gown was fitted in Memphis, Tennessee, at the Peabody Hotel.

"I will look forward to wearing your gown, Mama Lillian," Laura breathlessly replied. Lillian said, "Its fitted bodice features a portrait neckline, a full bouffant skirt, and handmade Alencon Lace, a needle lace originating in Alencon, France. It is often called the "Queen of Lace." "It will be perfect for you, Laura."

Amanda, Lillian, and Laura sat for a long time getting to know each other better while starting to plan what would be the wedding of the decade in Blue Mountain, Mississippi. A verbal smorgasbord of ideas floated through the air like butterflies lighting on a surprising, awe-inspiring occasion to occur in early May when Amanda's favorite daffodils will cover the hilltop surrounding the stately Greek Revival home.

Amanda reviewed the variety of narcissus perennials covering their hilltop, "Oh, yes, we will see Giant Star Daffodils; Petticoats; and even double Daffodils called "Tahiti" – all perfect for a happy wedding day. Plus, we have planters of Stephanotis, the delicately perfumed white flowers that are usually in wedding bouquets."

"We will have to ready tents for the big front lawn just in case of showers!" Lillian intoned. I heard landscapers from Philadelphia, Pennsylvania, came to Mississippi to suggest the perfect flora and fauna for this historic site in the 1940s.

Amanda replied, "Yes, indeed, I have the original hand-drawn plan in Grandmother's desk. They planted 'Rose Creek' Abelia to grace the front entrance. Their fragrance is similar to jasmine."

"We are already ahead of our plans– we must plan a wedding announcement for newspapers– the Tippah County newspaper, the *Southern Sentinel*; the *Tupelo Daily Journal,* and of course, both Memphis newspapers, the *Commercial Appeal* and the *Press-Scimitar*", Lillian proposed.

"I want to invite everyone in Tippah County to our wedding followed by a beautiful reception," Laura enthused. "How about close friends and family for a quiet outdoor ceremony and every one possible for a celebratory reception?" Amanda said decisively. "No, ma'am, Mama, everyone must feel welcome."

Suddenly, a whiff of cigar smoking and chuckling male voices came through the door. Drew sighed a mischievous smile, "Where have you been all my life, lovely Laura." A becoming blush lit her heart-shaped face as she whispered, "Waiting for you to find me …."

The group bid each other goodnight with plans to meet again for an old-fashioned Southern breakfast before work and play on Monday. Excitedly, Lillian mentioned bringing the one-of-a-kind wedding gown, veil, and wristlet.

An aura of well-being surrounded Laura and Amanda as their newly found family additions departed.

A genuine hug from Amanda thrilled Laura. “This is my best hug ever Mama. I am finally going to become a Southern Belle. I mean – a happy belle, Mama.”

Laura could not see Amanda’s tear-filled eyes as she left for her bedroom.

Before slumber, Amanda thought of how dramatically and positively their lives were changing. Then she wished for Tom to be a part of a newly found family life.

The next day at lunch with dearest friends, Waymon and Sarah Emma Cother, Amanda whispered the wedding secret, proposing the date and wanting to walk Laura down the aisle by herself. The dear old friends were surprised, enthused, and ready to assist.

Waymon Cother had more news to share, “Amanda, I found Tom living in New Orleans with a friend and writing transcriber, Pedro Santos y Gonzalez while writing his play, *A Streetcar Named Desire.*

The real streetcar named "Desire" was always on its daily route directly by their apartment in the French Quarter. Amanda gasped, "Thank you, Waymon, my dearest darling friend."

"We arranged for the duo to come from New Orleans for the wedding. I will pick them up in Memphis at the train station."

"I will keep this extraordinary 'gift' from Laura. She will be ecstatic and deeply appreciative and I will, too, Waymon."

Chapter 4.

LAURA WINGFIELD WEDS ANDREW CRAWFORD

ON a sun-dappled late April afternoon with daffodils dancing in the breeze on Hutchins Hill, Amanda Wingfield, proudly walked her pretty, fragile daughter, Laura, down the path from the front porch of their classical Greek Revival 1877 home pausing in front of Reverend Billy Bowen waiting by a pair of 1890 egg-and-dart tall English urns overflowing with white Phalaenopsis orchid branches, Bells-of-Ireland and white hydrangeas to wed Andrew 'Drew' Crawford her very first real gentleman caller.

"Here Comes the Bride" played softly as a child's tender voice sang:

> Here Comes the Bride~
> All dressed in white~
> Sweetly Serene in the soft, glowing light.
> Lovely to see~
> Marching To Thee'
> Sweet Love for Eternity.

Amanda quietly stepped aside to sit by Waymon Cother, Sarah Emma Cother, and Tom Wingfield with Pedro, his writing transcriber.

The Crawfords, a prominent Ashland, Mississippi, family, and the Hutchins, a prominent Blue Mountain, Mississippi, family, were delighted by this surprising pairing of a sought-after bachelor and a shy young woman.

A pearl-gray silk *crepe de chine* vintage Balmain sheath dress, found in her grandmother's closet, fit Amanda perfectly. The mother of the groom, Lillian Crawford, selected a pale blue silk organza jacket and a pencil skirt designed by New Albany, Mississippi, native Gayle Kirkpatrick, who took New York City by storm with his inimitable fashion creations.

Laura's only bridesmaid, Belinda Crawford, wore pale rose silk taffeta with the same portrait neckline and full flounced skirt that complemented Laura's dress style.

The gathered crowd was taken with Laura's newly found self-confidence as she floated on air to join her husband-to-be, Drew Crawford, looking beautiful wearing an ivory silk taffeta dress with twenty silk taffeta flounces, a choker of graduated South Seas pearls and a diminutive diamond bracelet.

After the longest kiss in Southern wedding history, Drew and Laura Crawford walked straight to the reception tent filled with well-wishers, abundant floral bouquets, and a four-foot-tall wedding cake ordered from the Peabody Hotel in Memphis and dozens of other gourmet foods.

Suddenly, "Unforgettable," sung by a Nat King Cole impersonator lured the couple to the small dance floor as Drew sang right along.

As a surprise, Tom Wingfield cut in on Drew as Laura shouted with joy. "Tom, my Tom, I love you and missed you every day after you left." Tom quietly said," Hush, Laura, I am here to celebrate." They were a sight to behold and they dance like the old days in St. Louis. Laura's slight limp was not pronounced.

As their toasts concluded, happy tears were shed by many, especially, Amanda Wingfield, who never expected love and marriage for her unusually sensitive daughter Laura.

Amanda told Waymon, "This is a fairytale. Thank you for bringing us home." She spoke quietly to Laura, "You look like an angel. I am so proud of you, Laura."

Laura cooed, "Dreams come true, Mama."

Amanda was calmer than ever due to the steadying influence of Waymon Cother.

Amanda stood close by Waymon, her childhood friend, and former gentleman caller. He whispered, "Amanda, you are as pretty tonight as you were when I was first in line as one of your many gentleman callers." Amanda smiled wistfully saying, "Waymon, I wish we could turn back the clock."

"No, dear one, this is as it should be for, I will always remain your most devoted gentleman caller."

A bell tinkled to summon the merry-makers for a final toast with Waterford deep champagne coupes filled with Piper-Heidsieck, the favored champagne choice of Marie Antoinette.

Lifting his champagne coupe, Drew toasted, "To Laura, the girl I chose to be my wife now and forevermore."

Laura rejoined, "To Drew, my one and only love and dearest gentleman caller."

The couple slipped into the home to change to traveling attire for tonight's short trip to The

Ripley Inn on the Square, an elegant renovation of a former large feed store. Each suite was luxurious and well-decorated with Italian Pratesi linens and a small side room stocked with homemade caramel cake along with a coffee pot ready for morning departures.

Tom and his friend, Pedro, elected to stay at home with Amanda until an early morning departure to Memphis to board the train to New Orleans with Drew and Laura.

The newlywed Crawfords fell into a quiet slumber before an early wake-up call to travel to Memphis to board the train immortalized by the jazz great, W. C. Handy, "The Fastest Train Out of Memphis." The Memphis-New Orleans line went through Batesville, Mississippi, to New Orleans.

The train wasn't full. Drew took Laura's tiny hand in his saying, "Darling, let's rest a bit until our arrival. Laura nodded, placing her lovely feathered beret-style hat on her lap while resting her head on his shoulder.

Tom and Pedro were on board a few rows back-sound asleep. They would all part company upon arrival in New Orleans.

Train time flew as they heard the conductor's voice suddenly announce, "Ladies and gentlemen, this is your conductor letting you know we will be safely arriving in New Orleans in ten minutes." Astonished to realize they slept the entire journey, Drew and Laura sat up, rested and eager to see The Crescent City.

"Drew Crawford, you are changing my life completely." He beamed, "Laura Wingfield Crawford, it is my greatest pleasure."

Tom and Pedro hurriedly passed by the couple saying, "*A bientot* (see you soon) and call us when you are lonesome!" Everyone laughed!

A nattily dressed driver was by the train exit with a large placard saying, "Crawfords" Laura was delighted saying, "Look Drew, we are famous!" Their baggage gathered, the twosome was not prepared for the true charm of the Crescent City. By North American standards it is a captivating old city loaded with history, jazz and blues, gumbo, Sazeracs, cemeteries, and music playing from daylight until dark.

All Laura could manage to say was, "Oh, Drew, at least a dozen times *en route* to the posh, historic Monteleone Hotel right on Royal Street in the renowned French Quarter. The hotel was built in 1886 in Beaux-Arts style for the Monteleone family who remain its proud owners after generations.

Laura gasped as they passed the Monteleone Grandfather Clock, hand-carved by Italian sculptor Antonio Puccio in 1909. It has become a meeting place before entering The Carousel Bar with its revolving seats priced at $100. per person. Laura was spellbound, ecstatic, and beautiful. Drew said, "Kid, you ain't seen nothing yet. We'll start to explore after checking in."

"Drew, Mama and I read every day and night while sequestered in St. Louis. Frances Parkinson Keyes wrote, "Dinner At Antoine's" about a famous restaurant here. Is it here?"

"Yes, darling one, we will dine at Antoine's and tour their wine cellar while we are visiting–they've been open since 1840, Laura." He continued, "We will visit the Beauregard-Keyes home where Ms. Keyes wrote right here in The French Quarter."

When the couple entered their well-appointed hotel room, they immediately spotted a huge bouquet of fresh flowers including the famed Blush Pink Honeymoon Roses and a bottle of *Blanc de Noir*, a sparkling Pinot Noir wine with a pink hue. They were surprised and delighted to have a toast leading to a 'nap' together. The card read, "… from Waymon and Amanda, with love forever."

After time spent in a romantic 'escapade,' Drew held Laura close declaring love. She cried out, "Drew, this is the happiest I have ever been. I don't ever feel lonely—not even for my beloved glass menagerie!"

A horse-drawn carriage with a coachman awaited the couple as they exited the fine hotel for a French Quarter Tour. Drew wanted her to see the architecture, the wrought iron balconies with abundant flowers, the courtyards, and ... first of all, the Ursuline Convent started in 1727 when a group of nuns from Normandy went to New Orleans to found a convent, run a hospital and take care of young girls.

As they entered the convent seeing beautiful gardens, unusual architecture, and an air of deep serenity, Laura gasped, "Drew, this is the most important place to me. Let's stay awhile."

He knew she longed for the sanctity and peace of the convent.

Only one more day left to explore before heading home to Blue Mountain, Drew said, "Laura, let's slow down.

We will return to New Orleans often. Now, we will walk to the famous Cafe du Monde where you will fall in love with beignets!"

"What?" she said giggling!

Off they went to eat this light, powdered donut style confection with Cafe au Lait, New Orleans rich, dark chicory coffee with real cream."

As they covered their faces with powdered sugar, they impulsively kissed to the applause of passing tourists. "Let's stay one more day, Drew, " she implored. "No, dear one, we need to go home. We'll always return.""

After a sound sleep, the newlyweds awakened in the historic Monteleone Hotel in the heart of the French Quarter of New Orleans due to the unexpected clip-clop sound of horses lining up in front of the hotel for carriage rides. Drew suddenly took time for another romantic 'escapade" delighting Laura.

"Today, Mrs. Crawford, we will hail a carriage after indulging in a sumptuous breakfast at Brennan's, a family-owned world-renowned restaurant for over seventy-five years. Are you hungry, darling?"

Laura enthused, "I am starving, Drew!"

They dressed hurriedly but, fashionably: Drew in a striking Brioni sports coat from Italy with side vents, a fine cotton lawn casual shirt, and no tie. Laura selected a Fifties-style full-skirted rose cotton dress similar to the glamorous actress Grace Kelly. Beyond their fine attire, they both looked ecstatically happy. "We are on Royal Street so, let's walk to Brennan's. The hotel concierge made a reservation for breakfast," Drew stated. "What? I never heard of having a reservation for breakfast, Drew!"

Off they went through the revolving door holding hands while standing as close as possible to each other. They were so absorbed in being together, that no notice was taken of people smiling as they passed by. Arriving at Brennan's renowned for its authentic Cajun and Creole cuisine, Laura gasped over the pink stucco facade with its distinctive gold letters spelling, Brennan's.

The hostess welcomed them warmly and checked their reservation while sending her assistant to show the charming couple to the coveted terrace area for brunch. As they were seated, Laura marveled at the celebrity turtles in a small pond nearby named after five French sauces, Bechamel, Hollandaise, Espagnole, Tomato Velouté −plus, Bordelaise, the only male. "How will I ever explain this magical city, Drew?" she whispered.

He said, "You will start a diary for our children when we arrive home. my love."

The charmingly attentive waiter took their order of Eggs Hussarde and softly scrambled eggs with truffles to go with a special glass of Barnaut Grand Brut Rosé champagne. Everything was superb including the famous flambéed Bananas Foster dessert.

Laura was completely transfixed by this extraordinary world. "Drew, you are spoiling me and changing my life every moment supreme," she whispered.

"A fine compliment that deserves a public kiss," he whispered as he leaned over to kiss her.

While on the luxurious, renowned Royal Street after the sumptuous meal at Brennan's, Laura was led by Drew to the redoubtable, magnificent antique purveyor, M.S. Rau. Entering Drew whispered, "Here we are in Ali Baba's irresistible cave, Laura." Speechless, she stood looking over the riches in the store known as one of North America's most respected high-end antique purveyors of jewelry, art, and antiquities since 1912.

The global company led by third-generation family member, Bill Rau, Drew called earlier to preplan a surprise for Laura—an Art Nouveau Perfume Flacon completely enveloped in silver. The store gift-wrapped the fine piece earlier for Laura to take home to Blue Mountain, Mississippi. Its hinged lid would keep liquids safe. A bottle of *L'Heure Bleue* by famous French perfumers, Guerlain was included. In 1912, Jacques Guerlain created the fragrance, "The sun has set, but night has not yet fallen. Time is suspended … in a moment when man finally finds himself in harmony with the world and light."

The saying was written on the enclosed card from Drew.

Unchecked tears streamed down Laura's pretty face. "This is a real-life fairytale, Drew Crawford. I am your Cinderella lost in the most splendid moments of love."

The elegant staff was touched by the scene. They had known Drew Crawford since boyhood when he came to the store from Ripley, Mississippi, with his family before Christmas.

His Father always found the most special presents for his Mother, a lifelong tradition revisited.

Off they went to the final stop on the fascinating shopping spree: Yvonne LeFleur, an internationally renowned custom millinery. Upon entering the most feminine shop imaginable, Laura was speechless. They were welcomed warmly and offered tea or wine. Laura whispered, "Oh, Drew, I wish Mama could be here right now." He smiled saying, "We will find a great hat for Amanda."

After the most fun trying on flattering hat styles, Laura departed with a classic black fedora for winter fashion and fun plus, a floppy fine straw hat for Spring with a silk grosgrain band and tiny curlicues of small silk daisies with a matching yellow silk band perfect for Amanda.

Just a few hours of quiet time in the elegant hotel induced the pair to make sweet tender love before departure. Laura and Drew were unaware this intimate occasion would result in twins nine months later. They hurriedly rose from their reverie to gather everything for the bellman coming to help them into a taxi heading to the train station.

En route, Drew sadly said, "It's time to say '*au revoir*' to this one-of-a-kind city, my darling Laura." "Do not be sad, Drew Crawford. You have introduced me to another world. I am not sad at all. I love you more and more, if possible." Yet another embrace and kiss followed her words.

During the train ride north toward home, the couple fell into a welcome sleep. Waymon Cother was to pick them up at the train station in Memphis. His Woodie wagon was really getting to be a taxi service. Off the train to meet a beaming Waymon, a usually modest gent, who hugged both of them at the same time. Laura chattered nonstop almost all of the way to Blue Mountain. Waymon was charmed by her enthusiasm and good story-telling technique.

Rolling up the long driveway to the house, the trio quietened.

Amanda sprang from the home holding what seemed to be a raccoon. "Welcome home, my darlings! Here's our new baby, Charlsie, a Maine Coon Cat, surrendered to a local shelter. Waymon brought him here to live with us!" His name was Charlie? That was too common for this handsome fellow with a huge plumed tail. I re-christened him Charlsie."

Laura exclaimed, "He's a four-legged masterpiece, Mama." Waymon says he weighs twenty pounds plus, the award-winning writer, Ernest Hemingway, has Maine Coon cats in his Key West, Florida, home." They invited Amanda into the outside dining room for tea, but she was too besotted with her new feline to accept.

Laura prepared a favorite Earl Gray Twining's tea on a tray with fresh garden mint and lemon wedges. "Your Mama is updating me about serving pieces, Drew. This tiny fork has three tines, because it is for lemons."

After reminiscing for a happy hour about New Orleans, the threesome heard a hair-raising screaming from the lower porch outside Amanda's room. The dining room kitchen was close by.

They raced from the dining room to see Amanda Wingfield standing by the outside door, alight with fiery flames licking her dress-ing gown like a raging bonfire. Drew ran quickly for water.

Immediate action by Waymon telling Drew to grab blankets from the stack waiting to be do-nated. Drew threw the blankets one by one roll-ing Amanda into the stack to douse the fire. He shoved Laura to the outside dining room to call the police for help and their family friend, Dr. Jessie Mauney, the only doctor in the area.

As the flames subsided, Amanda Wingfield lay unconscious and unrecognizable. Laura in complete shock, returned trying to tell them others were on their way.

When the flames subsided, Amanda lay unconscious and unrecognizable.

Drew, Laura, and Dr. Jessie Mauney loaded Amanda into the Woodie wagon to race to Memphis to The Med Burn Center. There was no air transportation or ambulance for this emergency.

Not a word was spoken beyond, Laura's whispered prayers. Waymon's face was awash with tears as he futilely denied this horror, "No-no, it's all right. Everything will be all right. We must race to the center in Memphis."

He and Drew made a stretcher of blankets to carry Amanda to the wagon. The police arrived sounding their siren. "We will accompany you all of the way to Memphis, sir. Push the speed to its limit."

There was no air transportation or ambulance in the town. Shock and despair kept the speeding wagon passengers quiet. The hospital was called to alert the staff of an emergency.

After what seemed to be a long trip, Waymon's Woodie squealed to a halt at the emergency door of The Med where attendants were waiting. The siren ceased bleating. All of the group realized it was too late to be all right. Doctor Mauney whispered, "There is a heartbeat. Let us hope and pray." Her wounds from burns were monstrous.

Only Waymon was able to speak calmly to the attendants. The wagon was permeated with the smell of charred flesh, blood, and death's imminent arrival.

Laura asked for permission to see her Mother for a moment before she was taken from the ICU. Drew Crawford listened at the door hearing her say, "You saved my life, Mama. I could not save you. I will speak of you fondly daily and think of you every morning. I will never forget how brave you were in St. Louis and how you somehow brought us home. So long for now, Mama ~ not goodbye."

By the power of God and sheer will to live, Amanda Wingfield waged a valiant 24-hour battle with the sneak and thief, "Death' overtaking her just as she was starting a new life in the beloved White House on a hill in Blue Mountain."

Chapter 5.

The Goodbye

HUNDREDS of villagers from Blue Mountain and others from Tippah County and surrounding towns, all races and sizes and religions, gathered on a rain-soaked early May day to bid "so long" to one of their favorite ladies as the Reverend Billy Bowen somberly addressed the mourners on the lawn of Hutchins House to say goodbye to Amanda Wingfield.

Tom Wingfield arrived from New Orleans as quickly as possible to be at his Mother's funeral. He was somber and saddened to know she died in such a horrible way. He told Waymon and Laura privately, "Not a day goes by when I do not know how much Mama wanted us to be well and happy."

Waymon's loving speech about Amanda always wanting all of them to be "all right' fell on deaf ears.

They would miss her and speak of her fondly for a long time.

By request, Reverend Billy Bowen read the poignant poem marked placed in Amanda's Bible: "We All Return To The Place Where We Were Born," by Oscar Gonzales.

The lovely remembrances closed with "Do Not Stand By My Grave and Weep" by Mary Elizabeth Frye.

Do not stand at my grave and weep,
I am not there, I do not sleep.

I am a thousand winds that blow.
I am the diamond glint on snow.
I am the sunlight on ripened grain.
I am the gentle autumn rain.

When you wake in the morning hush,
I am the swift, uplifting rush
Of quiet birds in circling flight.
I am the soft starlight at night.

Do not stand at my grave and weep.
I am not there, I do not sleep.
(Do not stand at my grave and cry.
I am not there, I did not die!)

The gathering remained still even though it was raining.

Amanda's simple oak casket was lowered into the ground of the red clay hills of Mississippi.

At dusk, a supper would follow in Amanda's honor to say, "So long, not goodbye to their very own daughter of the South."

Epilogue

Laura Wingfield Crawford, her beloved glass menagerie; her beloved husband, Drew, and Charlsie the cat, remained in residence in the big white house on a hill in Blue Mountain, Miss.

At dusk after the funeral, a time Amanda called the "blue hour" twilight, a supper was served for family and close friends in the outer dining room of the big white house on a hill.

Tom Wingfield and his devastated sister, Laura, took turns ringing the old dinner bell outside the outdoor dining room, a family mealtime tradition.

As time flew by, Drew Crawford followed in his father and grandfather's footsteps at their staid family bank and, as a community leader.

The entire county was delighted with the news of the arrival of their twins who were expected in January. Potential names were bandied about. Drew and Laura decided on Waymon and Amanda if it 'fit''. It did.

Babies Waymon, and Amanda arrived during the New Year's celebration much to the joy of family and residents of Tippah County, Mississippi.

A toast of Perrier-Jouet champagne was proffered by Waymon Cother honoring Amanda:

"To my small role as a devoted gentleman caller for the most charming southern beauty in Tippah County, Amanda Wingfield, who had at least seventeen gentlemen callers every Sunday afternoon.

"Amanda Wingfield had a brand of charm no other lady possessed, the rare gift of making everyone feel they were the most interesting, important person in the world.

"She never expected her new life to end tragically.

"Sometimes, Tom and Laura felt badgered by her desire for "the best" for them. This was born of love and was all she knew about being a Mother. She did not want them to be denied their rightful heritage.

"I loved her truly and she knew it without need of the words being spoken."

Made in the USA
Columbia, SC
05 March 2024

abe645a8-d5ef-4354-934c-4793fffc332aR01